There's an ELF IN YOUR BOOK

Written by TOM FLETCHER

Illustrated by GREG ABBOTT

For Buzz, Buddy and Max – T.F.

For Annika – G.A.

PUFFIN BOOKS

UK | USA | Canada | Ireland | Australia | India | New Zealand | South Africa

Puffin Books is part of the Penguin Random House group of companies whose addresses can be found at global.penguinrandomhouse.com.

www.penguin.co.uk
www.puffin.co.uk
www.ladybird.co.uk

First published 2019
This edition published 2020

003

Illustrated by Greg Abbott

Printed in China

A CIP catalogue record for this book is available from the British Library

ISBN: 978-0-241-35734-7

All correspondence to:
Puffin Books, Penguin Random House Children's
One Embassy Gardens, 8 Viaduct Gardens, London SW11 7BW

OH LOOK!

There's an Elf
in your book!

Elf's here to do the Nice List Test with you.

(You need to be on the Nice List if you want Santa
to bring you Christmas presents!)

To pass the test, Elf will ask you to do some **NICE** things . . .

But **WATCH OUT!** Elves can be a bit cheeky!

Don't be tricked into being **NAUGHTY**, OK?

When you're ready to take the test,
turn the page.

Good luck!

Let’s start with a nice easy one.

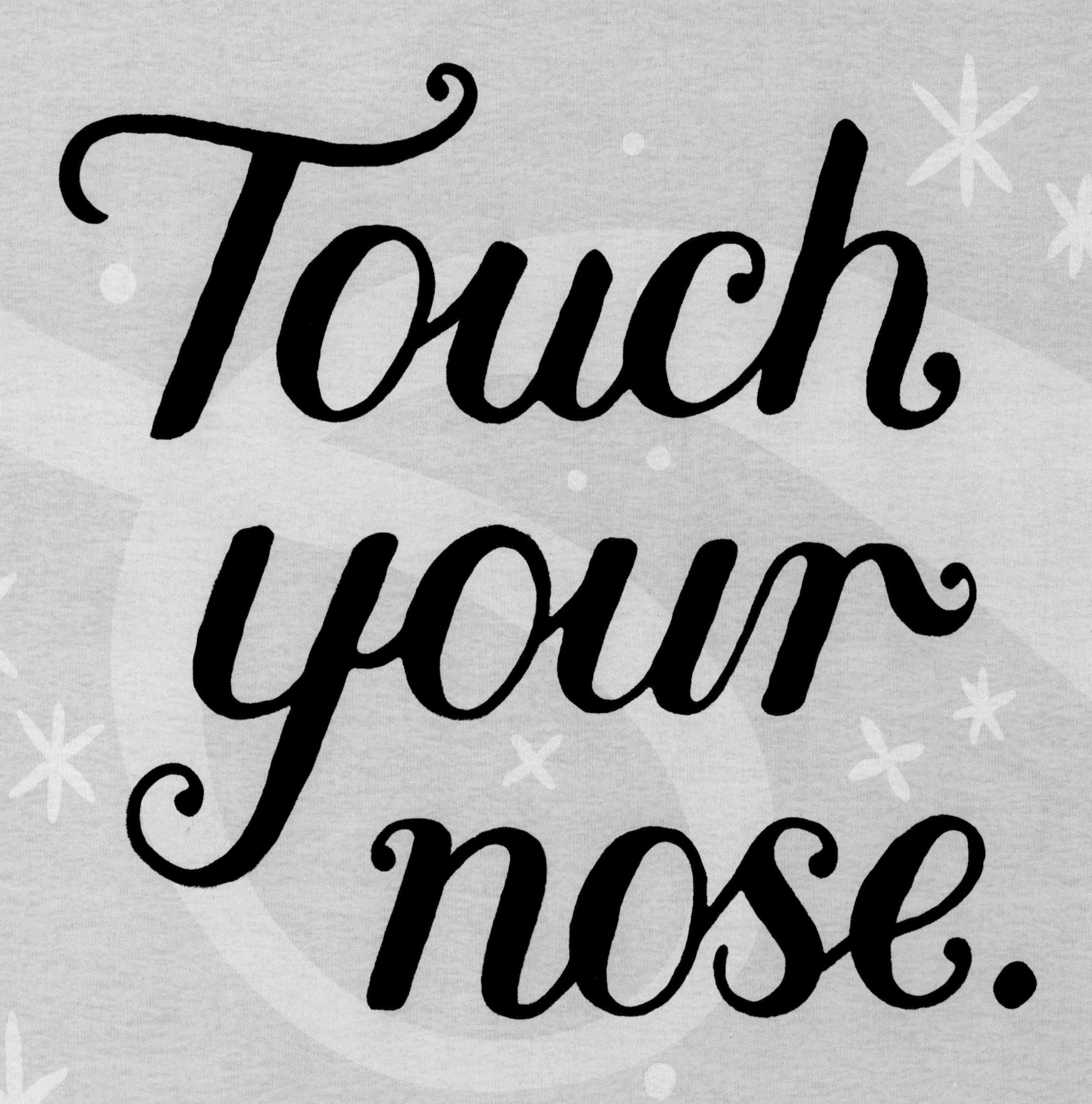

To see if you passed the test,
turn the page . . .

Good job! You passed the first test.
Now . . .

Blow a Christmas kiss.

Do you think you passed?

What a lovely Christmas kiss!
You passed the second test. What's next . . . ?

Sing a cheery Christmassy song.

Let's see if you passed . . .

Beautiful singing!
You passed the third test. Now . . .

Say, "I'm a bauble-bottom sprout face!"

Wait a second – this sounds like a naughty trick!
I think Elf is testing you.

DON'T say, **"I'M A BAUBLE-BOTTOM SPROUT FACE"** and turn the page . . .

PHEW! It *was* a trick.
Thank goodness you didn't say it.
You passed the fourth test.

Is the Nice List Test
going well so far, Elf?

Yes, it is!
Awesome! Keep it up.

Name
Santa's
most
famous
reindeer.

RUDOLPH! Correct! You passed the fifth test. You're great at this. Now . . .

EWWW!

STOP, STOP, STOP!

Do you think this is another cheeky elf trick?

It *was* another trick – well spotted!
Keep this up and you'll be on the Nice List in no time!

What's next, Elf?

Now for the final test . . .

Well, to make Elf laugh you'll have to tell a joke.
Have a look in the Christmas Joke Book.

Turn the page to open it.

There's a
CHRISTMAS
JOKE
IN YOUR
BOOK

WHAT
DO
Elves
DO IN THE
TOILET?

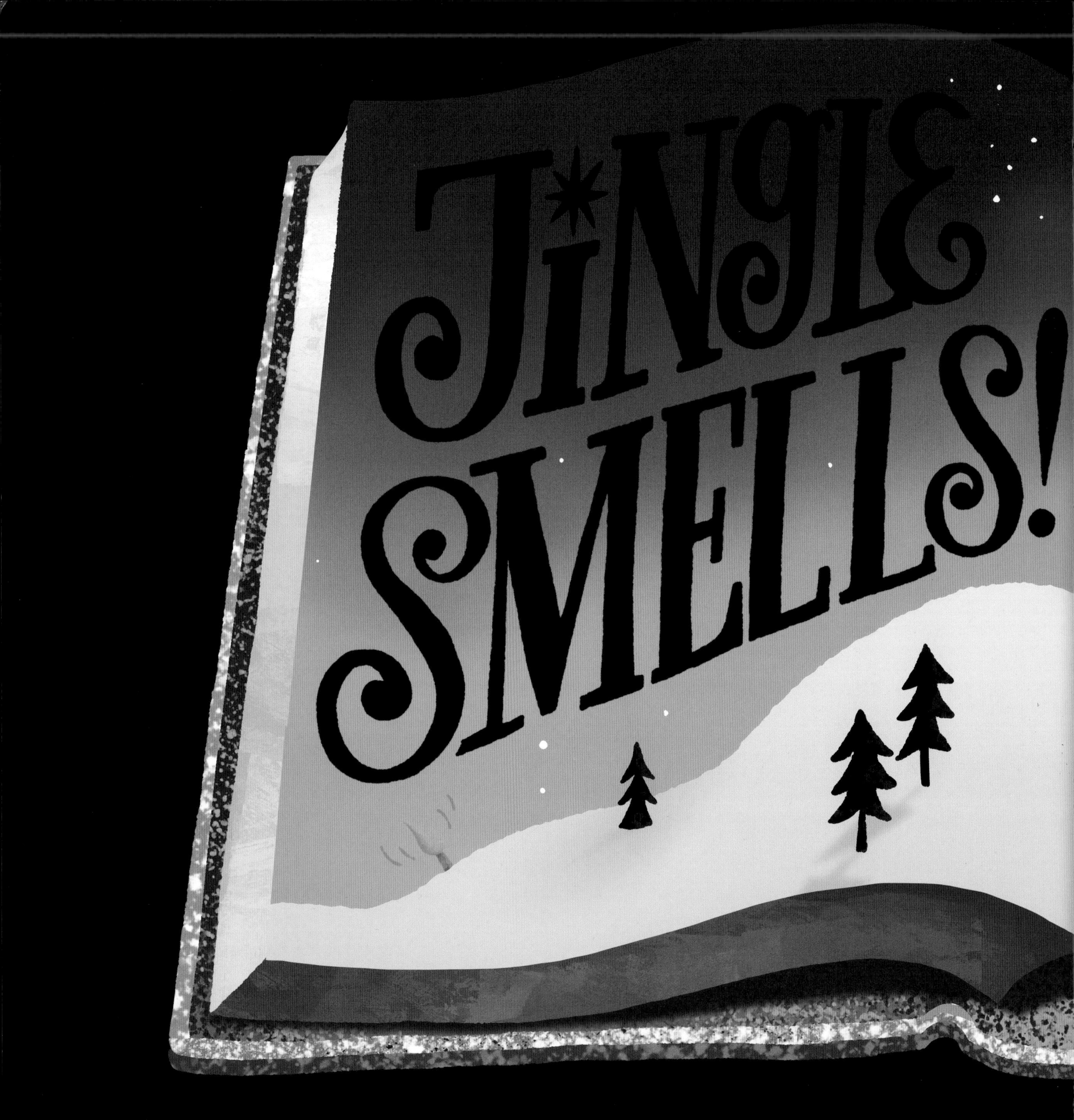
JINGLE
SMELLS!

Oh No!

The joke was a cheeky elf trick to make you say something naughty!

Does this mean you failed the test . . . ?

Surely you can't be on the Nice List if you've done something naughty.

It looks as though Elf feels bad for tricking you, but rules are rules . . .

Hang on just a second!
The test was to make Elf laugh
and **YOU DID**, so . . .

You passed the Nice List Test!

Well done!
You are officially on the Nice List.

And look – what's this?

WOW, it's your

Make sure you leave this book out on Christmas Eve – Santa will want to check it.

Until then, Merry Christmas.
STAY NICE!

BY Elf